And if I have prophetic powers,

and understand all mysteries and all knowledge,

and if I have faith, so as to remove mountains,

but have not love, I am nothing.

◆

—I CORINTHIANS 13:2

REVISED STANDARD VERSION OF THE BIBLE

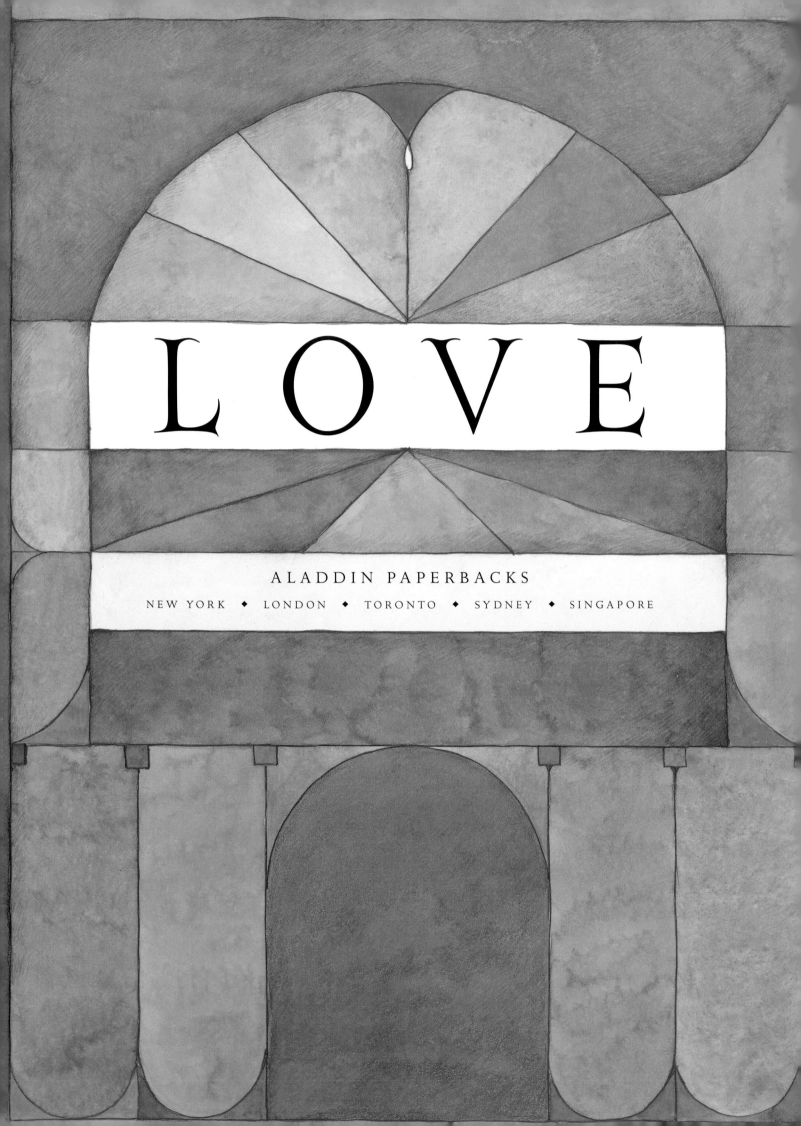

LOVE

ALADDIN PAPERBACKS

NEW YORK ◆ LONDON ◆ TORONTO ◆ SYDNEY ◆ SINGAPORE

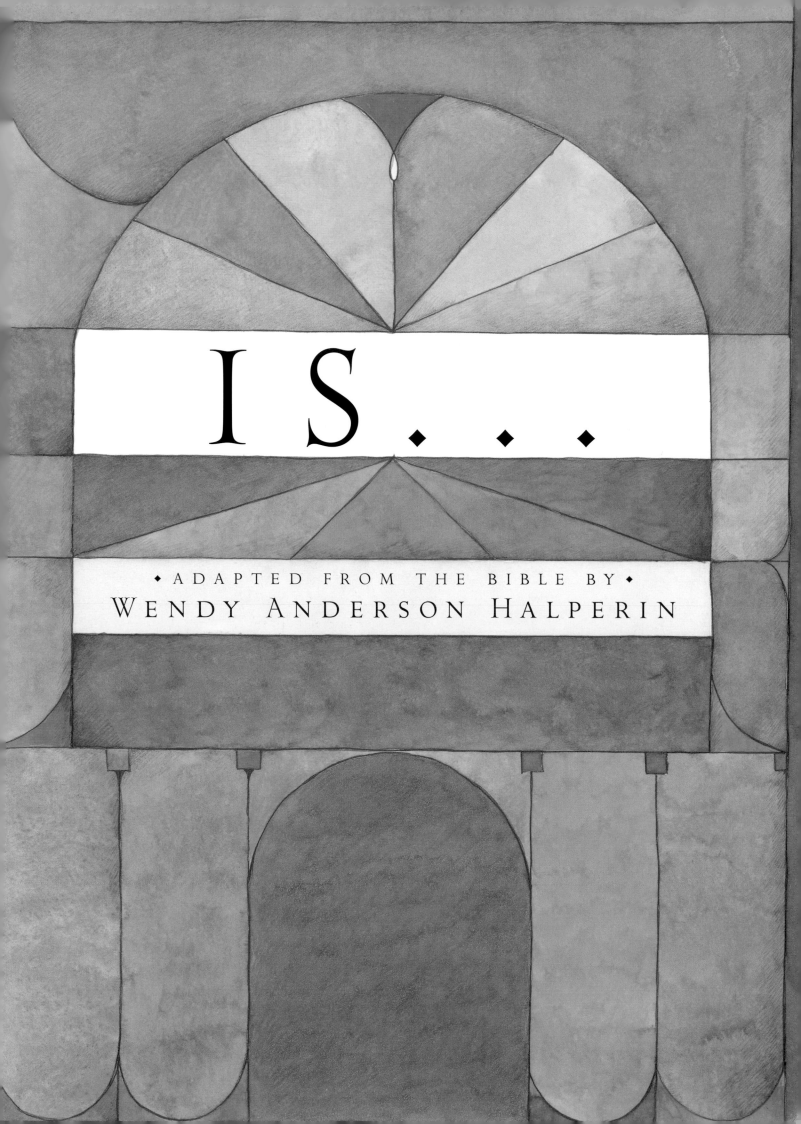

IS . . .

◆ ADAPTED FROM THE BIBLE BY ◆
WENDY ANDERSON HALPERIN

OVE . . .

IS PATIENT. LOVE IS KIND.

OVE . . .

IS NOT ENVIOUS OR BOASTFUL.

OVE . . .

IS NOT ARROGANT OR RUDE.

OVE . . .

DOES NOT INSIST ON ITS OWN WAY.

OVE . . . .

IS NOT IRRITABLE OR RESENTFUL.

OVE DOES NOT REJOICE IN WRONGDOING,

BUT REJOICES IN THE TRUTH.

OVE . . .

BEARS ALL THINGS.

OVE . . .

BELIEVES ALL THINGS.

OVE . . .

HOPES ALL THINGS.

OVE . . .

ENDURES ALL THINGS.

OVE NEVER ENDS. . . .

This book is dedicated to:

the apostle Paul,
Kevin Lewis & his mother,
Heather Wood,
Billie Dalton,
Chuck Fullar,
Inez & Carolyn,
John Mooy,
Mom & Dad,
Kyle, Aaron, & Kaleb,
Mrs. Penn,
Deborah & Donovan,
Julie, John, Paula, & Wayne,
Zoe,
Kale, Joel, & Lane,
Chelsie,
Craig & Pedro,
David (while he cut my hair),
Mark & Poe,
the home schoolers from Kalamazoo,

and you.

— WAH

◆ *A Note from the Illustrator* ◆

To create the illustrations in this book
I used pencil and watercolors. The ideas for the
numerous scenes depicted on each spread came not only
from me, but also from my children, our friends, and our
relatives. I loved illustrating these words, and if there's
one thing I've learned from the experience, it is that how
we respond to any person, any object, any situation is our
choice. We can choose to approach these things with
envy or arrogance, impatience or selfishness . . .

. . . or we can choose to act with love.

First Aladdin Paperbacks edition January 2004

Copyright © 2001 by Wendy Anderson Halperin

ALADDIN PAPERBACKS
An imprint of Simon & Schuster
Children's Publishing Division
1230 Avenue of the Americas
New York, NY 10020

Also available in a Simon & Schuster Books for Young Readers hardcover edition
Designed by Heather Wood with Wendy Anderson Halperin
The text of this book was set in Golden Cockerel and Cochin.

Manufactured in China
2 4 6 8 10 9 7 5 3 1

The Library of Congress has cataloged the hardcover edition as follows:
Bible. N.T. Corinthians, 1st, XIII, 4-8. English. 2000.
Love is / illustrated by Wendy Anderson Halperin.
p. cm.
ISBN 0-689-82980-9 (hc.)
l. Halperin, Wendy Anderson. II. Bible. N.T. Corinthians, 1st, XIII, 13. English. 2000. III. Title.
BS2673.C4   2001   242'.5--dc21   99-20337   CIP

ISBN 0-689-86675-5 (Aladdin pbk.)

◆ A Note on the Text ◆

What is love?
The apostle Paul attempted to define the word
for the followers of Christ living in the Greek city of Corinth in 56 A.D.
Almost two thousand years later, one part of his definition has come to exemplify
ideal love for countless people the world over. Often referred to as "The Way of
Love," Paul's words in I Corinthians 13 have been translated (and retranslated)
from Greek into a host of different languages. But no matter how many times
these words are translated, their essential message—that the love we express
is best defined by our attitudes and actions—remains constant.

For this abridged version of "The Way of Love," several English translations
of the Bible have been consulted. They include the King James Version,
the Holy Bible, New International Version,
and the Revised Standard Version.

And now these three remain:

faith, hope, and love.

But the greatest of these is love.

◆

—I Corinthians 13:13

Holy Bible, New International Version